NORTON AND Alpha

SIMON AND SCHUSTER
London   New York   Sydney   Toronto   New Delhi

NORTON WAS A COLLECTOR.
BATTERED WHEELS, RUSTY COGS, BROKEN SPRINGS —
THEY ALL FOUND THEIR WAY INTO NORTON'S COLLECTION.

BUT BEST OF ALL WERE THE THINGS NORTON **DIDN'T** HAVE A NAME FOR.

NORTON FOUND INTERESTING THINGS
ALMOST EVERYWHERE HE LOOKED.

THEY WERE RARELY BEAUTIFUL BUT THEY WERE USUALLY USEFUL.

AND FROM WHAT HE FOUND,
BIG OR SMALL,
NORTON MADE THE MOST
AMAZING INVENTIONS.

ONE DAY NORTON FOUND
SOMETHING INTERESTING
HE COULDN'T NAME.

HE ATTACHED IT TO
HIS LATEST PROJECT...

AND THEN STOOD BACK.

IT WAS **PERFECT!**

WOOF!

NORTON DECIDED TO
CALL THE PROJECT **ALPHA**.

NOW NORTON HAD A COMPANION TO HELP WITH HIS COLLECTING.

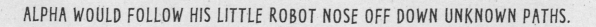

ALPHA WOULD FOLLOW HIS LITTLE ROBOT NOSE OFF DOWN UNKNOWN PATHS.

HE DUG HOLES, SCURRIED INTO SMALL, UNREACHABLE PLACES,
DELVED INTO UNEXPLORED SPACES...

...AND FOUND ALL SORTS OF WONDERFUL THINGS.

ONE TUESDAY MORNING,
ALPHA'S NOSE FELT SLIGHTLY ODD.
IT TICKLED AND TINGLED AND LED HIM
TO SOMETHING **VERY** UNUSUAL.

NORTON WAS BAFFLED.
IT WAS UNLIKE ANYTHING
THEY HAD EVER SEEN BEFORE.

BUT WHAT WAS IT?

NORTON AND ALPHA WERE DETERMINED TO FIND OUT.

SO, WITH A BIT OF EFFORT, THEY PICKED IT...

... AND SET OFF ON THEIR WAY HOME.

NORTON HELD ONTO **IT** TIGHTLY.

HE DIDN'T
TAKE HIS EYES
OFF IT
FOR A MOMENT.

EXCEPT
TO CLIMB
THE LADDER
UP TO
HIS HOUSE.

NORTON WENT STRAIGHT
TO HIS WORKSHOP.

STUDYING
THE
UNKNOWN

HE DID ALL HIS USUAL EXPERIMENTS.
HE OILED IT.

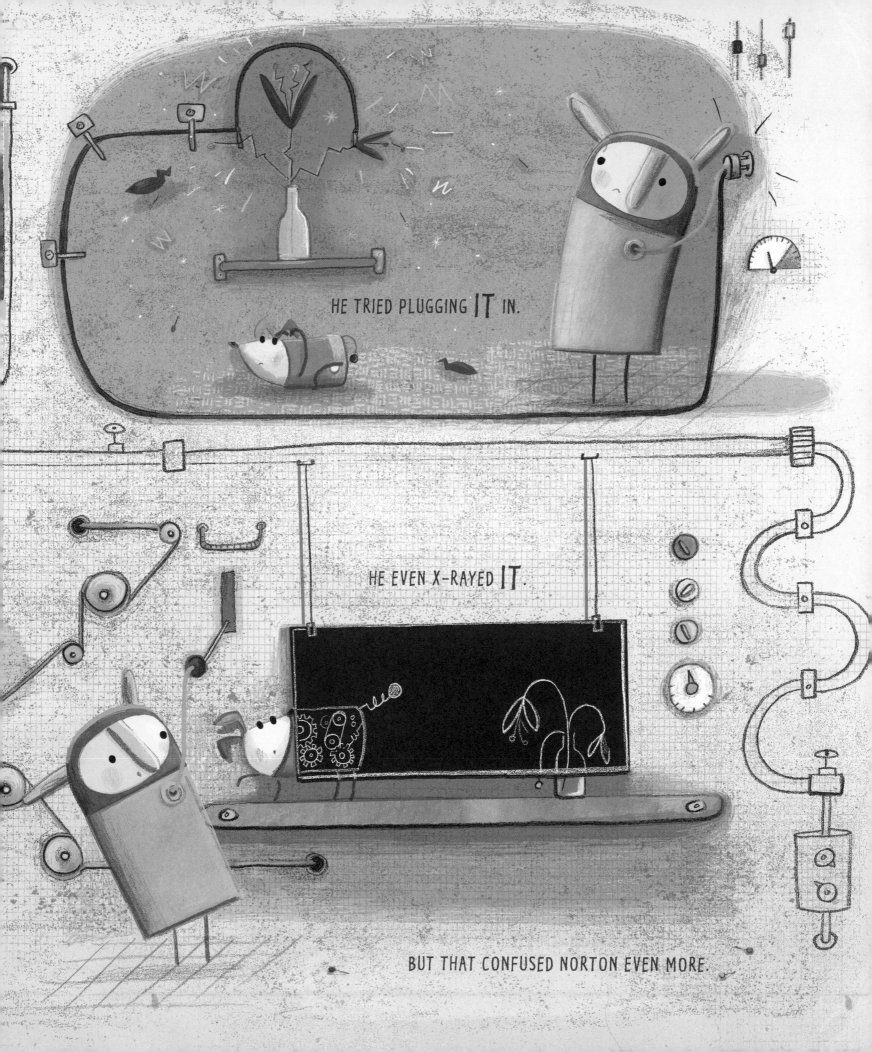

HE TRIED PLUGGING **IT** IN.

HE EVEN X-RAYED **IT**.

BUT THAT CONFUSED NORTON EVEN MORE.

IT DIDN'T SEEM USEFUL AT ALL.

IT ALSO DIDN'T LOOK NEARLY AS INTERESTING

AS IT HAD WHEN THEY'D FIRST FOUND IT.

SO
NORTON
THREW IT
OUT OF
THE
WINDOW.

FOR THE REST OF THE DAY, NORTON AND ALPHA
TIDIED UP THE MESS LEFT OVER FROM
THEIR EXPERIMENTS.

THEY FOUND A
LITTLE ROUND SOMETHING
THAT IT HAD LEFT BEHIND.

NORTON DECIDED TO KEEP IT.
MAYBE ONE DAY HE WOULD FIND
A USE FOR IT.

ON WEDNESDAY
IT WAS FAR TOO WET
TO GO OUT COLLECTING.

BUT ALPHA STILL NEEDED HIS EXERCISE!

ON THURSDAY
IT WAS EXTREMELY HOT.
NORTON AND ALPHA SPENT
MOST OF THE DAY TRYING
TO KEEP COOL.

BUT ON FRIDAY IT WAS A PERFECT DAY FOR TREASURE HUNTING.
THE WEATHER WAS GLORIOUS. SO NORTON MADE SURE THEY HAD A HEARTY BREAKFAST.

THEN HE OILED THEIR JOINTS
AND GOT EVERYTHING READY FOR
A LONG DAY'S COLLECTING.

THEY RAN TO THE DOORS
AND FLUNG THEM OPEN.

NORTON AND ALPHA BOUNCED AND JUMPED AMONG THE FIELDS OF ITS.

THEY COLLECTED UP LOTS OF ITS AND CARRIED THEM HOME.

NORTON FORGOT ABOUT TRYING TO FIND OUT WHAT IT WAS,
OR WHAT IT WAS FOR. BUT ONE THING HE DID KNOW WAS...

ITS MADE
HIM SMILE!